Annie and Snowball and the Prettiest House

The Second Book of Their Adventures

Cynthia Rylant
Illustrated by Suçie Stevenson

Ready-to-Read
ALADDIN PAPERBACKS
New York   London   Toronto   Sydney

To my goddaughters, Sarah and Audrey—C. R.

For Edwina and John—S. S.

ALADDIN PAPERBACKS
An imprint of Simon & Schuster Children's Publishing Division
1230 Avenue of the Americas, New York, NY 10020
Text copyright © 2007 by Cynthia Rylant
Illustrations copyright © 2007 by Suçie Stevenson
READY-TO-READ is a registered trademark of Simon & Schuster, Inc.
ALADDIN PAPERBACKS and related logo are
registered trademarks of Simon & Schuster, Inc.
Also available in a Simon & Schuster Books for Young Readers
hardcover edition.
Designed by Jessica Sonkin
The text of this book was set in Goudy.
The illustrations for this book were rendered in pen-and-ink and watercolor.
Manufactured in the United States of America
First Aladdin Paperbacks edition October 2008
4 6 8 10 9 7 5
The Library of Congress has cataloged the hardcover edition as follows:
Rylant, Cynthia.
Annie and Snowball and the prettiest house/Cynthia Rylant; illustrated by Suçie
Stevenson.
p. cm.
Summary: In the not-so-pretty house where she lives with her dad and her bunny,
Snowball, Annie plans to make some changes in the décor with the help of her
next-door neighbor and cousin Henry and his big dog, Mudge.
[1. Interior decoration—Fiction. 2. Friendship—Fiction. 3. Helpfulness—Fiction.]
I. Stevenson, Suçie, ill. II. Title.
PZ7.R982Anp 2007
[E]—dc22
2006023064
ISBN-13: 978-1-4169-0939-2 (hc.)
ISBN-10: 1-4169-0939-7 (hc.)
ISBN-13: 978-1-4169-1460-0 (pbk.)
ISBN-10: 1-4169-1460-9 (pbk.)
0714 LAK

Contents

Plain Things

Annie and her bunny, Snowball,
lived in a house next door
to Henry and his big dog, Mudge.
Henry was Annie's cousin.

5

He was also her best friend.
He taught her how to play Frisbee.

He showed her how to
make a knot.

He even helped paint
her dollhouse.

7

And Henry never made fun of Annie.
He never made fun of her
lace hankies or her frilly dresses.
(Annie liked dainty things.)
Henry was the best friend ever.

Annie liked Henry,
Annie LOVED Mudge,
and Annie liked living next door.

There was just one thing Annie
didn't like: her house.
It was a nice house.
It was a clean house.
But it wasn't a pretty house.

And Annie loved pretty things.
Annie lived with her dad,
and he wasn't very good
at making things pretty.

11

Annie looked at the plain couch
and the plain tables and
all the plain things her dad had.
And she wanted *pretty*.

So one day when Annie and Henry
were sitting in Henry's backyard,
Annie told him about what she wanted
(while Mudge drooled on Snowball's
head).

13

"You should go through
our attic," said Henry.
"We have tons of pretty things.
Stuff from grandmas and lots of aunts."
"Really?" asked Annie.

"Sure," said Henry. "You could borrow
things for your house."

"*Really?*" Annie asked again.

Mudge came over and sat on Henry.
Henry groaned.
"Would you like to borrow
a dog, too?" he asked.
Mudge just licked him.

Annie picked up Snowball and smiled.
She was finally going to have
a pretty house.

Wonderful Things

Annie and Henry got permission
from Henry's mom to go
through the stuff in the attic.
"Just don't take Dad's tuba,"
said Henry's mom with a smile.

Henry and Mudge and
Annie and Snowball climbed
the stairs to the attic.
"Wow," said Annie.
"Your attic is big!"

She looked over into a corner.
"Look at that pink lamp
with the beads!" she said.
"I love it!"

Snowball had already found a
box to explore.
Mudge was exploring a shoe.

"Here's a crazy quilt," said Henry.
"And look at this fancy mirror."

"Wow!" said Annie.
She saw a flowered chair
in another corner.
"Perfect!" she said.

"Hey," said Henry, "here's my old crib."
Annie looked at the crib and imagined
Henry in it.

Then she imagined *Mudge* in it.
She giggled and giggled,
imagining Mudge.
"What's so funny?" asked Henry.
Annie told him.
Henry thought it was funny too.

Mudge just ignored them.
His shoe was too good.

28

Annie found wonderful things
in Henry's attic.

She went home and told
her dad all about them.
She asked if she could change their
plain house to a pretty house.

Annie's dad was a good dad.
"Sure," he said, "but can I
keep my beanbag chair?"
Annie smiled and hugged him.

A Pretty House

Annie and Henry and Henry's parents
and Annie's dad all helped
carry pretty things out of the attic.

They carried lamps and chairs.
They carried tables and mirrors.

They even carried a lovely old angel
with a chipped wing.
Annie loved her the best.

Then everyone moved the
plain things out and the
pretty things in.

It took moving this and that
to here and there
to get it all just right.

But when they were finished,
Annie's house was beautiful.
"Wow!" said Henry.
"Where's the butler?" asked Henry's dad.
"I *love* it!" said Annie.

Everyone celebrated
with ice-cream sundaes
at Annie's new kitchen table.

Snowball got a pistachio nut.
Mudge got all the cherries.
And everyone agreed:
It had been a very *pretty* day!